LAND OF THE KANGAROO PEOPLE

BY PERCY TREZISE

Angus&Robertson
An imprint of HarperCollins*Children's*Books

This saga, JOURNEY OF THE GREAT LAKE, is dedicated to my colleague of many years, Aboriginal author and artist Dick Roughsey. It is also dedicated to all my Aboriginal friends who led me through their temples of Dreamtime, passing on the legends and stories of their race memory, which records their history back through countless millennia, recalling the dramatic humid and arid weather phases of the Ice Age.

The saga is set circa 30,000 years ago to encompass the extinct megafauna of marsupials, reptiles and birds, the giants of Dreamtime, which shared this ancient land with the people of those times.

Percy Trezise

Angus&Robertson
An imprint of HarperCollins*Children'sBooks*, Australia

First published in Australia in 2001
This edition published in 2015
by HarperCollins*Publishers* Australia Pty Limited
ABN 36 009 913 517
harpercollins.com.au

HarperCollins*Publishers*
Level 19, 201 Elizabeth Street, Sydney NSW 2000, Australia
Unit D1, 63 Apollo Drive, Rosedale, Auckland 0632, New Zealand
A 53, Sector 57, Noida, UP, India
1 London Bridge Street, London, SE1 9GF, United Kingdom
2 Bloor Street East, 20th floor, Toronto, Ontario M4W 1A8, Canada
195 Broadway, New York NY 10007, USA

National Library of Australia Cataloguing-in-Publication data:

Trezise, Percy.
Land of the Kangaroo people.
ISBN 978 0 2071 9938 7 (hbk.)
ISBN 978 0 2071 9992 9 (pbk.)
1. Aborigines, Australian – Legends – Juvenile literature.
I. Title. (series: Journey of the Great Lake; 6).
398.20994

Colour reproduction by Graphic Print Group, Adelaide, South Australia
Printed and bound in China by RR Donnelley on 128gsm Matt Art

INTRODUCTION

Aboriginal oral history tells of hundreds of Dream Roads criss-crossing
the Australian continent which were made by Ancestral Beings during their travels
at the beginning of Dreamtime. It also tells of a vast freshwater lake
at the top of Australia and stories about ancestors like the Anta Moola sisters.

There is also scientific evidence to suggest that 36,000 years ago there was a large
freshwater lake at the top of Australia. Scientists called it the Lake of Carpentaria …
and it was also known as Balanorga, the big water.

This is the story of three children and their journey around Balanorga,
along the Dream Road of the Anta Moola sisters, to find their way home.

Percy Trezise
Cairns, Queensland
2001

The Kadimakara children had been resting on the island for a few days, fishing by night and hiding and sleeping by day, when late one afternoon their dingo, Lasca, woke them by growling. Peering through reeds they saw a group of the Kangaroo cannibal people had come to camp opposite them. They had dingoes, and all the dingoes were looking across to them.

Jadianta told the others to lie still and quiet and wait until dark when they would take to their raft and flee. As soon as the day faded he swung his bullroarer so the Kangaroo People would think their dingoes had seen Quinkins on the island and would be too frightened to come over and see their tracks.

There was no moon and when it was fully dark they put their things and Lasca on their raft and pushed off, paddling quietly away.

When they came to a river running into the lake they decided to row up the river, before leaving their raft to travel overland back from the lake shore where there were too many people. They still followed the Sister stars.

They travelled at night and slept by day, in the light of early morning or evening they found nonda trees with ripe yellow plums and filled their dillybags. Lasca used to go hunting early every morning after they found a safe hiding place for the day, and usually returned with a small wallaby, possum or bandicoot, which cooked in a ground oven while they slept. When they woke they ate the meat and continued their journey.

One morning Lasca was out hunting, watched by other animals, when a large marsupial wolf saw the young dingo and decided to have her for his breakfast. He bounded out from among bushes to chase and catch her.

Marsupial wolves bounded like big cats and were very fast, easily outrunning a dingo.

But Lasca knew instinctively how to evade the wolf bounding after her. When the wolf was about to grab her in his jaws, Lasca folded her legs and rolled sideways.

The big wolf, who couldn't stop or turn quickly, rushed past her and Lasca got up and ran off in another direction, with a fresh start on the wolf, zig-zagging toward camp and the protection of Jadianta's spear.

Lande saw Lasca coming, pursued by the wolf, and called Jadianta to get his spear, grabbed her digging stick and ran out to hit the wolf.

Lasca rolled near them, Lande threw her stick at the wolf and Jadianta hit him in the shoulder with his spear. The wolf ran away and Lasca was safe but bleeding from two wounds.

Lasca was hurt and could not hunt, so each morning Jadianta took his boomerangs and spear to find food. One morning he saw Bulinmore the echidna, which was nice and fat, but Jadianta knew the laws, the echidna could only be eaten by father's father.

He went on toward a big lagoon, hoping to get some ducks or other water birds.

There were lots of ducks and geese on the water and when they flew up he threw his boomerangs among them. The returning boomerang was a good weapon; if it hit a bird, they fell together, if it missed, the boomerang returned to be thrown again.

Jadianta was very pleased when he got two fat magpie geese.

They kept travelling at night and found a *walpa* to cross any big rivers, leaving the *walpa* on the far side where the owner could easily find it.

They kept their direction by following the Sister stars.

They had just woken up late one afternoon when Lasca growled to warn them that people were coming. Jalmor pointed to a party of Snake Men coming along following their tracks. Jadianta called to the others to gather their things and run.

Wongabel, the little Jabiru girl they rescued from the Snake Men, was terrified and ran fast with them.

The Kaidaicha Man, an appointed executioner, was out on a mission for the elders. When he reached the edge of the plateau, he looked down and saw the four children running with their dingo. He recognised Wongabel as the young girl stolen from his tribe by raiding Snake Men.

He also saw the Snake Men, and recognised the leading man to be the one he had been sent to kill.

He set off to lope along and get ahead of the children.

The Kaidaicha Man wore emu-feather slippers to disguise his footprints and had been highly decorated on his back and face to show his official position and hide his identity.

He went past the children then hid behind an ant bed to watch them pass.

When the running Snake Men came in sight the Kaidaicha stood up and hurled a heavy spear into the chest of the leading man. He went down screaming, the rest of the Snake Men stared in horror at the dreaded Kaidaicha Man, then turned and fled.

The Kaidaicha Man walked slowly after the children, his mission complete.

Jadianta was surprised that the Snake Men had not caught up with them, he did not know about the Kaidaicha. Late next evening they arrived at the camp of Wongabel's people. Her parents were very happy to have her back.

After being swept from their home Jadianta, Lande and Jalmor have journeyed through many lands and faced many dangers. Reaching the land of the Brolga People they must soon walk up the other side of the lake to return to the Kadimakara People. Will Goorialla lead them safely home?

GLOSSARY

bullroarer
a small oval of wood with a string tied to a pole in one end, making a roaring noise when swung around the head

dillybags
woven grass bags for carrying food and belongings

Dream Road
the path of an Ancestral Being during Dreamtime

ground oven
a hole in the ground lined with stones which were heated by a large fire, after which the food was placed on the stones and covered over

Kaidaicha Man
An official executioner appointed by the elders to kill one judged guilty for a crime. Always intricately painted on back and face to hide identity, and wearing slippers of emu feathers to disguise footprints. The anonymous killer

nondas
plums of the nonda tree; yellow oblong fruit which were a staple food in northern Australia

Quinkins
supernatural beings wandering at night, some friendly but mischievous, others bad and evil

Snake Men
a clan who thought their ancestors were snakes

walpa
a raft